Jonathan Smyth

Cowboy Sleuth

BOOK SIX

The Case of the Murder Mansion

Frank F. Fiore

Jonathan Smyth

Cowboy Sleuth

BOOK SIX

The Case of the Murder Mansion

Frank F. Fiore

STORY BACKGROUND

THE SMYTH NOVELS ARE A NEW TWIST ON THE STANDARD WESTERN. THEY PIT THE BEST OF THE BRITISH AGAINST THE AMERICAN WEST, FILLED with action, drama, twists, turns, and gunfights.

Jack the Ripper is terrorizing the citizens of London, and there is only one connection between each murder known to the police - an amateur sleuth called Jonathan Smyth. After a particularly grizzly murder, the fickle finger of fate points directly at Smyth, who cannot be located. When Scotland Yard discovers that their prime suspect has seemingly fled to the fledgling United States, they send one of their best men, Charles Abbott, after him.

Smyth, an intrepid sleuth, is caught in a new land filled with legends, mysteries and horrors. His goal is to unmask the Ripper when he commits his gruesome and horrible murders again in the Wild West.

PROLOGUE

Buck Brannan leaned against the worn pew of the small chapel, his gaze fixed on the stained-glass window depicting a lone rider against a setting sun. His face, etched with lines from years in the saddle and kissed a deep brown by the desert sun, held a hint of impatience. It also wore an old scar that ran down the left side of his face - half closing his eye to his jowls - a testament to a past encounter, adding a touch of menace to his features.

"Tell me," he pressed. The question to Maggie Star, the young nurse's aide at the hospital, was less a request and more of a demand.

"Not here," Maggie replied, her voice low. She glanced around the empty chapel, her eyes darting towards the entrance. Buck's reputation wasn't exactly a secret. "There's a small cafe down the street. We can talk there."

A few minutes later, they were seated at a corner table, the soft hum of conversation providing a backdrop to their urgent discussion.

"Now," Buck said, leaning forward, "what did you find out? What was in that telegram?"

Maggie hesitated, her fingers tracing the rim of her coffee cup. "You were right about them. They're investigators chasing Jack the Ripper. The telegram was to Bess, a reporter with them. I couldn't hear the exact contents, but I overheard Bess exclaim that the lead pointed them to New York."

"New York?" Buck repeated, his brow furrowing. "That's it? Nothing else?"

"Yes. One other thing. They're going to look for a seaman there."

She paused, her eyes meeting his. "When do I get paid?"

Buck reached into his worn leather vest and pulled out a twenty-dollar gold piece. "Here." He tossed it onto the table. "And keep this to ourselves. This conversation never happened."

Maggie fingered the coin, a flicker of amusement crossing her face. "What conversation?"

CHAPTER ONE

Riding the Transcontinental Railroad, Smyth, Abbott and Bess arrived in New York in a few days, after traveling through inclement, cloudy weather.

"So, this lead we have," queried Smyth as they pulled into the Grand Central Terminal, "are you sure it's from someone credible?"

"I've known Don Jackson to be a reputable reporter," Bess said as they exited the passenger car and walked the platform towards the Lexington Avenue exit. "Reported on a case or two with him. If he says he's found something about the Ripper, we need to sniff it out. Let's get a carriage and head down to his office and see what he has."

As the inclement weather worsened, the three caught a horse-drawn coach, or a horse-bus as it was called, and they chose one of the two wooden benches along the sides of the passenger cabin. The driver sat on a separate, front-facing bench, typically in an elevated position outside the passengers' enclosed cabin.

"The weather here is a lot like London," Abbott noted, scanning the streetscape as they rode.

"Yes," Smyth added. "Feels like home."

"This is it," Bess chirped. "Coachman! Let us off here."

The three disembarked and Bess paid the fare. They entered the lobby of a four-story brownstone building and went to the visitor's desk.

 "Can you direct us to Don Jackson's office, please?" A short, plump, 50ish woman sitting behind the desk looked up. "He's expecting us."

She peered over her reading glasses and replied, "Fourth floor. City Desk. Take the elevator," pointing to her right.

Stepping into the elevator, Abbott remarked, "These are more advanced than the ones we have in England."

The spiffy looking uniformed elevator attendant asked, "What floor?"

 "Fourth," Bess replied.

A few moments later, they exited the elevator and walked through the glass doors marked 'City Desk', populated by rows upon rows of desks manned by reporters.

Bess singled out one of them. "We're looking for Don Jackson."

The reporter kept on typing, flicked his thumb over his shoulder and replied, "In the back. Corner office."

They were about to walk towards the back when a pair of burly arms came up from behind Bess and gave her a big hug. "Bessie! You got my telegram! Glad you came. It's been too long."

Bess pried those meaty arms from around her and replied, "Don. This is Jonathon Smyth and Charles Abbot. Jonathan and Charles, this is Don Jackson."

Jackson grabbed Smyth's hand and shook it vigorously, then slapped Abbott on the back. "Great to meet you two."

He paused a beat. "So, these are your new partners helping you find the Ripper, huh?"

Smyth bristled at this and his informality. "To be correct, sir, Bess worked her way into our investigation."

"Yep. That's my Bess," Jackson replied. "Sticking her Scottish nose into other people's business."

Sensing a change in the conversation, Abbott intervened. "You said in your telegram that you had information on the Ripper."

"Yes, and I do. Come to my office."

The trio followed, navigating themselves through the ocean of desks on the busy floor until they reached Jackson's office.

"You can leave your luggage here. Have a seat," Jackson said, then paused. "Hmm. It seems to be a chair short."

"I'll stand," Smyth replied. "This shouldn't take long. Just tell us what you know."

"Is he always this surly?" he asked Bess, then dismissed the thought. "Never mind."

"It's been a long trip," she said, "and a disappointing investigation, so please tell us what you have."

"While you were chasing ghosts out West looking for Ripper like murders," he began, "we had real murders with Ripper like victims right here in the East. A particularly horrible one right here in New York!"

"Like whom?" asked Abbott.

"Carrie Brown, a Bowery prostitute who was murdered and mutilated in a lodging house. She also went under the name of Old Shakespeare. Odd one she was. She got the nickname for her habit of quoting William Shakespeare during drinking games."

"Is this what you brought us all the way out to New York for?" Smyth said. "To tell us of a local prostitute's murder?"

Bess joined in." Yes, Don. Is this all you have?"

A smile crossed Jackson's face as he walked behind his desk. "You're gonna owe me for this." He opened the bottom draw to his desk and withdrew a beat-up police notebook. "This fell into my hands recently." He handed the notebook to Bess. "You should find it interesting."

"What is it?" she asked.

With a sly look on his face, Jackson replied, "It's a journal of a British police officer - his private notes about the Ripper murders."

"Where did you get it?" asked Smyth, now very interested.

"The person I got it from purchased it at a London Street Market and it found its way to me. I bought it as a possible source for a story that may be connected to the Carrie Brown case. But..." giving Bess the eye, "I thought of my old friend Bess. Figured I could bring back old times, uh, working together." He winked.

"You're such a luv," she winked back. "But those days are gone."

Jackson sighed. "It was worth a shot."

"Past nostalgia aside," interrupted Smyth, "what's in the notebook?"

"The police officer did mention a name in his notes. An American from New York. Jack Kelly. Even got an address for him here when questioned. But he couldn't be found to follow up further. So, they dropped him as a person of interest." He paused a beat. "That's it. That's all I have."

"An American, huh? That's quite interesting but pretty thin as a lead," Abbott remarked.

"Why didn't you pursue it here?" asked Smyth.

Jackson's eyes brightened. "I did. That's why I sent you the telegram. Sniffed around and found where he lived in the city." He looked at Bess. "Wanna partner on this one?"

"If necessary," she replied.

"Let's pay him a visit," Smyth said.

CHAPTER TWO

Smyth, Abbott, Bess, and their new partner took the elevator to the ground floor and hailed a two-horse drawn carriage. Seating only four passengers, it was much smaller than the horse-bus.

"Where to?" the driver asked, peering down through a rectangular opening in the front of the carriage. He sat in an elevated position outside the enclosed cabin.

Jackson informed him of their destination, and they were on their way.

"This has to be an improvement over those dusty old stagecoaches I heard about out West," Jackson remarked.

"Believe me," Abbott replied. "No contest. Rides better too."

As they passed a corner, they didn't notice the lean, rugged man in a worn Stetson and jeans, out of place in the cosmopolitan city. He approached a small, private, single horse-drawn coach.

It happened in an instant.

A man with a badly scarred face boldly stepped up to the carriage and grabbed the reins of the horse and the driver's whip. With a swift, expert flick of the whip, the horse bolted forward, its hooves kicking up dust as it raced down the cobblestone street.

"So where is this address you have?" asked Smyth.

"It's in Harlem," Jackson replied. He paused a moment and looked back over his shoulder. "Do you hear that?"

"What?" Abbott and Bess said in unison.

"Some crazy is racing a horse over the cobblestone street behind us." A beat later he added, "And coming up fast. Look!"

They all turned just as bullets peppered the coach.

"Get down!" yelled Smyth and pushed Bess to the floor of the carriage. Abbott screamed, "Bloody, hell!" and followed, landing on Jackson who was already face down with his head buried under the seat.

The coach then started weaving back and forth, tossing the passengers across the floor. Abbott looked up at where the driver was sitting and saw a bloody arm dangling through the rectangular opening.

The coach was swerving left and right, bouncing over curbs, smashing mailboxes, and barreling through outdoor cafés. The horses, spooked by the gunshots, were in full panic mode.

The coach was out of control.

"Our driver was shot!" Abbott cried.

"Get down!" cried Bess.

"Got to get to the driver's seat," shouted Smyth as he opened the door to the coach.

"You're crazy," yelled Jackson.

Smyth ignored him and proceeded to climb out of the carriage. The door rhythmically hit him on the back as it flew open and closed. He looked back over his shoulder to see the assailant that was shooting at them, but to his relief, he was not following them.

Hand over hand, Smyth managed to climb on top of the coach as it swayed violently under him.

By now, the wild, out-of-control coach had entered Central Park and began to career between boulders and trees, one time tilting on its two sidewheels, threatening to overturn, then the other. Smyth reached the driver's seat, pulled the wounded driver up and out of the way, and took control of the terrified horses.

But relief was short-lived. The wild ride shook the bolt holding the crossbeam attached to the horses, threatening to pop out. Smyth, holding the reins in his teeth, climbed down to the crossbar and banged on the bolt with his boots while the coach was still bouncing and swaying. Luckily, his efforts were successful, and the bolt popped back into place.

He then brought the runaway team back under control.

"What the hell was that?" cried a dazed Jackson.

"Um. Does this happen frequently in New York City?" Abbott asked. "We can get this kind of treatment out West!"

At that moment, a mounted NYPD officer rode up to the group. "What's happening here? Saw your coach careen through the Park."

"We were shot at!" cried Jackson, shaking from the experience.

"Shot at?" the officer replied.

"And the driver has been wounded," added Smyth. "He should be sent to a hospital."

"Of course," the officer replied. "And then you all come to the station, and we'll take your statements."

 "We shouldn't have left our sidearms in our luggage at Jackson's office," remarked Abbott. "Who thought we might need them in a modern metropolis."

CHAPTER THREE

After leaving the police station, Smyth, Abbott, Bess, and Jackson - still bewildered by the attempted murder - planned their continued trip to Harlem.

"We should go back to the hotel and grab our sidearms," Abbott suggested. "Just in case that killer shows up again."

"Not necessary," Jackson replied. "The police have been alerted. We'll use a conveyance with lots of people. Safety in numbers, as they say."

"Like what?" Smyth asked.

"We'll take the el," Jackson said. "It's slower, but we'll have to walk from the station anyway."

"The el?" Abbott questioned.

"The elevated rapid transit steam train," Jackson explained. "They run above the city streets, hence the name 'el.' There's a station nearby."

They followed Jackson to the towering steel structure and climbed the metal stairs to the wooden platform.

"How often do the trains run?" Bess asked.

"Pretty frequently," Jackson replied. "One should be here soon." He looked down the track and saw a plume of smoke approaching. "Here we go."

A series of carriage cars, pulled by a locomotive with a smokestack, chugged down the track and came to a halt.

A conductor opened the doors, inviting the four travelers inside. They took seats on the wooden benches. The car was well-lit with kerosene chandeliers and had wide windows.

"This is quite quaint," Abbott remarked as he settled in. The coach was nearly full of passengers returning home from work.

"I feel a lot safer on this," Jackson sighed. "If that madman shows up here, we'll have some protection from the crowd."

The ride was comfortable, and within an hour, they arrived at a Harlem station. "We walk from here," Jackson said.

As they walked through Harlem, they observed the neighborhood's diversity. A mix of old and new buildings lined the streets – tenements and brownstones.

After a twenty-minute walk, they reached a three-story tenement building. "This is it," Jackson stated.

They climbed the stone steps to the entrance hall and searched for the name "Kelly" on the building's directory.

"Right here. Down the hall," Jackson said.

A few minutes later, they were knocking on the door. An elderly woman peered through the chain link lock. She looked suspiciously at them and asked, "Who are you and what do you want?"

"I'm a reporter from the New York Post," Jackson replied. "We'd like to see Mr. Jack Kelly."

The old lady wrinkled her lip and said, "He's not here."

"Do you know when he'll be back?"

"He's ain't comin' back," she sneered.

"Never?" Bess said.

"And who are you?"

"I'm also a reporter. We really need to speak with Mr. Kelly. Do you know where he might be?"

A voice from behind suddenly appeared. "Who is it, mother?" said a middle-aged man.

"Some people looking for Jack."

"Well, let them in."

Reluctantly, she released the chain, allowing Jackson and the others to enter.

The middle-aged man led his guest to the living room. "Seat yourself. I'm George, Jack's brother, and this is Mabel, our mother."

"My name is Don Jackson, and this is Bess MacDonald, Charles Abbott and Jonathan Smyth."

With the pleasantries over with, Jackson got straight to the point. "We would appreciate any information you can give us on Jack."

"He was a sailor of some kind for most of his life," George began. "Perhaps all of it. We saw little of him. He worked on an assortment of cargo ships landing in ports throughout Europe."

Mabel interjected. "At least that's what his rare postcards said. One said he stopped in England for a while. Until a few years ago..."

George interrupted. "He ceased to follow the sea. But we saw and knew so little of him that we don't know where he went in the last few years."

"We think he was in Illinois and Wisconsin," Mabel said. "But don't know for sure."

"He was all over the West," George added, "and traveled a great deal." He paused a beat. "That's all we really can tell you. I'm sorry."

"Well, we thank you for at least seeing us and tell us what you know."

They said their goodbyes and exited the apartment.

"Now what," asked Abbott.

"I don't know," Smyth replied. "I'd like to get another look at those policeman's notes."

CHAPTER FOUR

A few blocks from the el, Smyth slowed his pace and moved towards Bess, nudging her closer. "We're being followed." he whispered.

She whispered back, "Who is it?"

"A woman. Don't turn around."

They continued walking, Smyth keeping a watchful eye over his shoulder.

Smyth moved up to Abbott. "Take Jackson and keep walking. We are being followed."

"Is it that madman? Do you see a gun?"

"No. A woman. Do what I say."

Smyth and Bess stopped, pretending to window shop. Abbott and Jackson continued walking.

The woman following them also stopped, a few yards behind.

"Grab my hand," Smyth said. "Let's cross the street and duck into that alley."

Down the alley they positioned themselves to be hidden behind some tall boxes but able to view the entrance of the alleyway.

And waited.

The female stalker followed Bess and Smyth across the street and entered the alley. When she reached Smythe and Bess, Bess jumped out from behind their hide and grabbed the woman from behind. "Gotcha!" she said pinning her arms behind her back.

Smyth came forward and asked the restrained woman, "Who are you and why are you following us?"

A few moments later, Abbott and Jackson came running down the alleyway.

"Who's the woman?" asked Jackson.

"That's what we're going to find out. Let her go, Bess." A beat later, he asked, "Now who are you?"

'I'm Jack Kelly's stepsister." She straightened out her clothes. "And we need to talk."

"Ok," Smyth replied. "Talk."

"Not here in the street. Is there someplace private we can talk?"

"We can go to my office," Jackson replied.

CHAPTER FIVE

Back in Jackson's newspaper office, Abbott took no time retrieving their sidearms from the luggage and handed Smyth and Bess's theirs. "Not going be caught without these again," he remarked, stuffing his pistol in his suit jacket.

They all took seats with Abbott and Smyth standing. "OK, Miss...Miss...?" began Smyth.

"Jennifer Kelly. You can call me Jen."

"OK, Jen. Let's talk."

"I assume," she began, "that you didn't get far with our parents."

"No," Jackson replied. "We learned very little about your stepbrother."

"Could you give us any further information?" asked Bess.

"Yes." she said. "I'm assuming that Jack has something to do with the Ripper in England."

"Why do you assume that?" Abbott replied.

"I know of the policeman's private notes describing the Ripper's murders and Jack being one of the suspects. But he disappeared when they tried to follow up on him with questions." She paused a moment to let her revelation sink in. "And have you figured out why Jack couldn't be found?"

"How did you know about the policeman's notes?" asked Jackson.

"I knew they existed and was about to obtain them when they fell into your hands, Mr. Jackson."

"But how did you know...?" Jackson replied.

Smyth interrupted, "What did you mean we should have figured out why he couldn't be found in England for more questioning?"

"My parents told you he was a seaman, correct?"

"Yes," Smyth replied. "Go on."

And that he shipped out to Europe – specifically one time to England."

Smyth nodded.

"My brother was a very disturbed soul, Mr. Smyth. Especially concerning women." She searched her jacket pockets and pulled out a small diary. "This is Jack's diary. He left it to me when he was home on one of his infrequent visits."

She opened it to a dog-eared page and read it to the group. "It says here in this entry, of his strong disapproval of the immorality of woman and his problems dealing with them. Primarily all kinds of "skanks" and of his having been on the "warpath" to make them pay for their sins."

"That doesn't prove he's the Ripper," Bess scoffed.

"Jack lists his port of calls. It states he landed in London on August 30th, 1888, and shipped out on November 10th, 1888. Are those dates familiar to you Mr. Smyth?"

"Yes. Those dates bracket the five murders committed by the Ripper."

"Mr. Smyth," she continued, "How can you ignore a theory that Jack was a merchant seaman who landed in London just before the Ripper murders started and left right after the last brutal murder. He boarded his merchant ship and returned to America to commit twelve hideous murders in five states." She showed the diary to the group. "Right here he lists the cities all pushing west." She turns to Jackson. "Look them up, Mr. Reporter. You'll find a Ripper like murder in each of these states. He lists them in this diary. All you have to do is confirm them."

"So," Jackson said, "are you saying that your stepbrother was responsible for the Ripper murders in London?"

"Yes. Then continued his murderous spree here in America."

Jackson added, "And started here with Carrie Brown in the Bowery."

Jen nodded.

"Does his diary say where he will commit the next murder," asked Bess.

"They are being committed as we speak," she replied. "In Texas"

"That's a bold statement," Bess replied.

"Can you confirm that, Jackson?" asked Smyth.

"Yes. I'll telegram our sister paper in Austin."

"If confirmed," Bess added, "we're headed back West.

"It'll be confirmed and when it is," Jen said, "I'm coming with you. I'll meet you at Grand Central."

CHAPTER SIX

The three men and Bess waited at the busy Grand Central train station for Jen Kelly to arrive when Smyth asked, "Did your Austin paper confirm the murders in Austin?"

"Yes," Jackson replied. "But that doesn't prove Jack Kelly is the Ripper or that the diary she has is legit."

"She knows too much," Bess added, "and I trust her too little." She paused a beat. "And she's hiding something to boot."

"Woman's intuition?" Smyth remarked raising an eyebrow.

"Don't knock it, luv." Bess retorted.

At that moment, Jen appeared with her sparse luggage.

"So," she began. "Are we confirmed about Austin?"

Jackson nodded.

"Good. When do we leave?"

"Lower level. Platform B. Track 2," Jackson replied. "Boarding now."

Several minutes later, they arrived at the platform and boarded their train.

Storing their luggage and taking their seats, Smyth asked, "So, Jackson, what did you find out about these murders in Austin? What did the newspaper tell you?"

"They've been reporting on the murders," Jackson replied. "It seems bodies, hideously and brutally murdered, have been showing up all over the city. Even letters were sent to the newspaper taunting the police to stop him."

Abbott remarked, "Remember the Ripper letters sent to the newspapers?"

"Yes." said Smyth. "Similar Modis Operandi. The Ripper's "Dear Boss" and "Saucy Jack" letters."

"What did they say?" asked Jen.

"The letters often boasted of the killings and taunted the police," said Smyth. "They also described the murders in graphic detail, suggesting a sadistic enjoyment of his work and mocking the police, and relishing the challenge of evading capture."

"Quite a piece of work, this psycho," Jackson remarked.

"We may be on to something," Abbott said.

Smyth nodded. "We might."

"How long to Austin?" asked Bess.

Jackson removed the train schedule from his pocket. "We'll be in Austin in three or four days. That gives us enough time to chew on all of this."

CHAPTER SEVEN

Their arrival in Austin was a stark contrast to the bustling metropolis of New York. The train depot was a modest wooden structure, bustling with activity but lacking the grandeur of Grand Central.

"Not exactly the city that never sleeps," Abbott remarked, lugging his suitcase down the platform.

"Let's catch some sort of transportation at the station and make it to the newspaper," Smyth said.

They collected their belongings and headed for the station exit where they hailed a horse-drawn carriage and provided the driver with the address of the Austin Daily Statesman. As they rattled through the city's dusty streets, Smyth couldn't help but notice the unique blend of frontier charm and modern progress.

As they left the train depot, they didn't notice a man with a badly scarred face hail a coach behind them - to follow.

"We going to see one of their reporters," Jackson said. "A Mike Owens. He'll fill us in on the latest news."

A half hour later, traveling through a city still filled with a frontier atmosphere, they arrive at The Austin Daily Statesman.

Jackson paid the driver and walked up to two-story brick and stone façade building.

"Still a rustic town," Jackson observed, "but growing in sophistication. Let's find Owens."

They found him, a tall, lanky man with a Stetson that seemed almost as big as his head. He greeted them with a warm handshake and a drawl that was thick as a Texas barbecue.

"So, you're the reporters from New York," he said. "Glad you could make it. Now who's Jackson?"

"I am," he said, extending his hand."

"Glad to meet a fellow 'stringer'. And who's this pretty lady here?"

"I'm Bess McDonald. I'm what you say "a stringer" too."

"Really! You don't say? A reporter."

"You have something against women reporters?" she furrowed her eyebrows.

"Nope. Nice to have a filly in amongst us." He looked at Jen. "And who's this other filly?"

"I'm Jen Kelley."

"You a reporter, too?"

Jen shook her head.

"Mr. Owens..." Smyth began.

"You're a Brit. Recognize the accent. Call me Mike. We're informal here out West."

"So we have discovered," Smyth replied. "Now what more can you tell us about these murders?"

"Brutal. Savage. And at the same time - odd."

"Odd?" Bess remarked. "What do you mean?"

"Well," Owens began, "The victims are all women. Prostitutes. Nothing odd about that. The animal doing this has it out for them. He said so in his letters to the paper's editor." He shook his head. "Sick bastard. Oh! I apologize to the ladies."

"Apology accepted," Bess replied. "Now what about the part being odd?"

"What's odd is that we are finding the bodies in different parts of the city," Owen continued. "Primarily in or around Guy Town. Located in the First Ward where prostitutes peddle their wares. We believe they are dropped off around Guy Town but killed elsewhere."

"They had to be killed in someplace private though, to be mutilated like that," Abbott said.

"Yes," Owned replied. "The bodies were sliced up pretty bad. Takes time to meticulously remove organs and such. Some bodies were even found burned." He paused a beat. "Wish I can tell you more, but we're as baffled as the police."

"Well, thanks for telling us what you know, Mike," Jackson replied. "By the way, we're hungry. Didn't eat much of that food they served on the train. Any suggestions for places to eat and a good place to sleep?"

"The Driskill Hotel. One of the most luxurious hotels in Austin. You'll like it there and the food at the restaurant is top notch. You can walk to it from here."

The five collected their baggage and set out for the hotel.

Owens wasn't kidding. The hotel was an elegant Victorian palace with a lavish interior design rivaling hotels in New York. They approached the registration desk and checked in. "Five rooms please," Smyth stated.

"Names please," the well-dressed clerk asked.

"Jonathan Smyth, Charles Abbott, Bess McDonald, Jen Kelly and Don Jackson," Smyth replied.

The clerk handed Smyth the room keys and said, "I'll have the bellhop bring your luggage to your rooms."

"Can you direct us to your restaurant?" asked Abbott.

"To your right and through those glass doors."

A few minutes later, the four were sitting at a table enjoying a tasty meal. After a much-missed repast, Jackson patted his stomach and said, "I'm pleasantly satisfied and beat."

"So am I," added Bess. "Too much traveling in too many days."

Bess and Jackson stood up, excused themselves, and made their way to their rooms.

"What about you Jen?" asked Jackson.

"I think I'll walk the town a bit. See you in the morning."

"Then it's just you and I, Abbott. Care for a night cap at the bar?"

"I'll pass. I shall retire. See you in the morning."

CHAPTER EIGHT

Buck Brannan, scratching the scar on his face, eyed Smyth from across the restaurant as he traveled to the bar. Passing through the glass doors of the restaurant, he made note of the possible rooms the five investigators had been assigned. He hoped to finish the job he started back in New York.

Knowing the rooms were on the second floor, he'd followed the bellhop with their luggage but couldn't determine the exact assignments.

He'd have to take a gamble.

Choosing a room at random, he drew his .45 Colt Peacemaker and knocked on the door.

A few seconds later, Bess opened the door, her face frozen in surprise at the sight of the gun pointed at her.

"What! ... What the ...!"

"Shut up," Brannan barked, grabbing her by the throat and pushing her roughly back into the room, tripping over a nightstand and sending a lamp crashing to the floor.

Brannan picked her up, holding her in front of him with the gun to her head. "Now. You're gonna tell me what you know about the Ripper. And where he is."

"Who are you?" Bess managed to cough and rasp out a question.

"I missed you in New York," he said. "You answer my question, or I won't miss you again," he threatened, pressing the gun harder against her temple.

He released his grip on her throat slightly, and she gasped, "What's Jack the Ripper to you?"

"The reward. A tidy sum."

"So, you're a bounty hunter!?" she exclaimed, shocked.

Just then, hearing the commotion from his room across the hall, Abbott burst into the room, his face a mask of confusion. "I heard ... what in bloody hell!"

Surprised, Brannan shifted his pistol from Bess to Abbott. "Get in here!" he waved his gun towards the bed, still holding Bess in front of him with one arm around her neck.

"What's this all about?" Abbott cried.

"You both are going to tell me what I want to know or..."

As if on cue, Jackson entered the room. "Bess. Your door was open, and I wanted to ask you..."

His attention diverted, Bess saw her chance. She grabbed Brannan's gun hand and bit down hard on his flesh.

He screamed in pain, firing his gun instinctively and striking Jackson, who collapsed to the floor. With his free arm, he threw Bess at Abbott, sending them both tumbling to the ground.

Fearing some had heard the shot from the bar, he ran to the stairs, almost bowling Smyth over as he barreled past him.

Smyth rushed into Bess's room.

"It's Jackson," Bess cried. "He's been shot!"

Abbott yelled, "The man with the scarred face! He shot Jackson. He just left!"

"I saw him on the stairs, heard the gunshot from downstairs" Smyth said.

"Get him, Smyth. Get him!"

CHAPTER NINE

Brannan, a blur of fury and desperation, barreled down the stairs, sending patrons sprawling in his wake. His escape was a chaotic ballet of panic and confusion, the lobby echoing with the sounds of startled cries and the clatter of overturned chairs.

Smyth burst into the lobby a few moments later. "Did you see a man run down the stairs" he shouted, his voice barely audible over the commotion.

"Yes," several guests replied, their faces still pale from the sudden chaos.

"Which way did he go?"

"He went out there. Out the back," an older gentleman said, picking himself up from the floor.

"Thank you," Smyth replied, and hurried out the back doors. The once-tranquil courtyard was now a scene of confusion by the hotel, but as he ran farther away the sound of Smyth's footsteps echoed against the cobblestones.

He paused in front of the stables, his ears straining to pick up any sound. Except for the gentle neighing of horses in their stalls, the air was eerily quiet.

He approached the stable doors, his hand reaching for the handles. Before he could pull them open, Brannan, riding a horse bareback, burst through the doors, throwing Smyth aside.

Smyth recovered, ran into the stable, chose a stall, threw a bridle on the horse standing there with eyes wide open, and mounted him bareback.

With a kick to the horse's ribs, he was off in pursuit of Brannan, who had ridden across the courtyard and into the lobby.

All hell had broken loose again in the lobby as Brannan frantically searched for a way out. Smyth's entry only added to the chaos - chairs, tables, sofas, and guests being tossed about as the horses, now in a state of panic, bolted from one corner of the lobby to another.

Smyth managed to maneuver his horse toward Brannan's, pushing them both against the tall glass lobby doors. With a sickening crunch, Brannan's horse fell through the broken glass, sending both him and the animal tumbling into the street.

"Got him," Smyth thought, a sense of relief washing over him.

But that was not to be. Brannan recovered, remounted his horse and took off.

Smyth, jumping his mount through the broken door, gave chase and slammed past a stunned Jen, returning for the evening.

"Smyth!" she gasped.

Smyth ignored her, his focus solely on the man fleeing before him.

The two horsemen tore through the town, kicking up a cloud of dust. In this frontier city, such a sight was not entirely unusual, but the intensity of the chase made it a spectacle to behold.

The chase continued for blocks. Smyth kicked his horse, urging it to gallop faster as the bigger horse slowly gained on the bounty hunter.

The wind whipped at their faces, blurring their vision, but Smyth refused to relent. His determination was fueled by a mix of adrenaline and a burning desire to bring Brannan to justice.

Several minutes later, the two horsemen approached the outskirts of the city and the railroad tracks. Smyth looked ahead, his heart pounding in his chest. An express train, its whistle piercing the air, was rapidly approaching to his right.

He saw Brannan steer his horse towards it - a reckless gamble that could end in disaster.

Smyth urged his horse forward. He was almost on the bounty hunter when Brannan, with a desperate leap, cleared the tracks right in front of the oncoming train.

Smyth pulled his horse to a hard stop. The train thundered past, its powerful engines shaking the ground. He stared at the spot where Brannan had disappeared.

Brannan had escaped.

Back at the hotel, Smyth headed to Bess's room when Abbott buttonholed him in the lobby. His anger and frustration were palpable.

"Jackson will be all right," Abbott said, trying to offer a reassuring smile. "He'll be in the hospital for a while."

Smyth couldn't hold back his fury over the incident and the loss of Brannan. "What the bloody hell is going on!?" he exclaimed, his voice echoing through the lobby.

"That man was the one who tried to kill us in New York," Abbott began, his tone serious. "He also intended to kill us if we didn't tell him what we knew."

"Knew what?" Smyth asked, his confusion growing.

"What we knew about the Ripper and where he was."

"Why?" Smyth pressed.

"He was after the reward posted for the Ripper in England." Abbott shook his head. "The man is a blooming bounty hunter."

"This case is getting stranger by the moment," Smyth replied, trying to make sense of the chaos. "All right. Let's collect everyone and plan tomorrow."

CHAPTER TEN

The next morning, the group gathered in the lobby of the Driskill Hotel, ready to begin their investigation. Smyth suggested they start by visiting the crime scenes. "We need to get a firsthand look at what we're dealing with," he said.

"Then we go to Guy Town," Abbott replied.

Guy Town was a bustling hub of activity, with brothels, saloons, and other entertainment venues catering to a variety of clientele. It was a place where people from all walks of life could find what they were looking for, whether it was excitement, companionship, or simply a place to escape the stresses of everyday life.

Owens had provided them with a list of the known locations, and they spent the day visiting each one in Guy Town.

"These crime scenes are worse than anything in Whitehall," Abbott remarked.

Smyth agreed. Blood and gore still stained the sidewalk.

"The air here is thick with the stench of decay," Bess remarked, holding a hanky to her nose.

Jen agreed, holding a piece of lacy cloth to her mouth also.

"I have a suggestion," Bess said. "Let's split up. I'll walk the area alone. Maybe I can draw the perp out."

Smyth didn't like that idea at all. "No. Too dangerous. I won't allow it."

This got Bess's Scottish up. "You won't allow it? Who are you to tell me what to do?"

Abbott jumped in. "Let's not fight. T'will get us nowhere."

Bess, still fuming, said, "We are at a standstill here! Do we visit each stinking site, or do we try something new? Besides, I can take care of myself. And if I get into trouble, I'll fire a shot from my sidearm."

Smyth was quiet for a beat, then said, "Don't wander far."

Bess winked. "Okay, luv."

The others split up. Smyth went alone, and Abbott went with Jen.

Bess walked the streets, keeping an eye on her back and scoping out the area. She didn't see the scarred figure darting in and out of the late afternoon shadows, following her.

She caught a glimpse of the figure and patted her sidearm on her waist just as a young woman suddenly crashed into her.

The woman was hysterical and started to run from Bess.

Bess grabbed her, shouting, "Wait! Wait! Tell me what's wrong!"

"Please let me go," the young woman pleaded, her voice trembling. "He's after me. I know it! That beast! I only just escaped," she cried, tears running down her face. "He was going to kill me!"

"Who?" Bess asked, trying to calm the woman.

"That horrible animal. Monster."

"Calm down, miss. Tell me. Slowly. What are you talking about?"

"The house." She pointed down the street. "The one behind those gates. He tried to kill me there."

She shook Bess off and ran frantically down the street.

Bess let the crazed girl go and cautiously walked to the house she pointed out.

She approached the tall metal Gothic gates and could see a very large Victorian mansion set back far from the street in a grove of trees. The three-story mansion, with its peeling paint, broken windows, and overgrown gardens, evoked a sense of foreboding and mystery.

Bess decided to investigate this find before calling in others on the team.

I shouldn't be doing this alone, she thought. But her competitive investigative instincts got the better of her.

She gently pushed on the gate and found, to her surprise, that it easily opened. She made her way down the stone path to the mansion and approached the front door. It was ajar. Probably from the girl who ran from the house, she thought.

She decided to take the easy entry to the property as an uninvited invitation and moved into the main hall of the mansion. The impressive walls rose all three stories of the building. Doors and archways leading into darkness surrounded her. Flickering dim illumination cast sinister shadows that seemed to be moving, undulating.

She unholstered her pistol and moved through the large entry hall that was dimly lit by oil lamps on the wall. Fifty feet in, she arrived at a set of tall twelve feet high double doors. She pushed them open to a small room that contained a short flight of stairs.

"That's odd," she wondered. "Such a small room and staircase in this big house."

She shrugged and climbed the set of stairs that led to a wall. The only way she could go any further was down a long, twisted and complex series of dark hallways to her right. "This is ridiculous," she mused after following this path for a short way, "I'm going back and get Smyth and the others."

It was not so easy to get back. The twists and turns she had taken in this maze of hallways now confused her. She could feel a sense of concern, then anxiety, pulling at her, which she fought hard to dispel. Finally, she reached a door. "This is the one," she muttered, "The one where I came in."

She pulled on the doorknob and suddenly, the floor opened under her feet.

Thirty minutes later, she awoke from her fall, tied to a chair. The tiny room she occupied was lit from a single oil lamp above her head. Her bare feet felt sticky from an unknown substance on the floor.

A shadow was cast from behind by the dim light. She tried to focus on the image, chasing the cobwebs from her mind, when a ghastly image materialized before her. She let out a horrifying scream when she realized the image was a figure. The figure was Buck Brannon. And he was hanging on the wall, disemboweled. His blood covered the floor and Bess's feet.

CHAPTER ELEVEN

"Nothing," Abbott remarked to Jen, his voice tinged with disappointment.

"Maybe Smyth and Bess had better luck," Jen said. She paused for a beat. "I'm thirsty. Let's find somewhere to get a drink."

Abbott and Jen turned the corner when they saw a young woman walking towards them. Her face was wide eyed and streaked with tears.

Abbott approached the woman and asked, "Are you all right, young lady?"

She just looked at him, tears welling up in her eyes, not saying a word. Then she looked straight at Jen. "You need to save her."

"Save who?" Abbott asked.

Jen offered her a handkerchief. "Here. Tell us. Who needs to be saved?"

She dried her eyes and said, "The Scottish woman. I think she was Scottish or British by her accent. I told her what happened to me and where." She blew her nose. "I'm pretty sure she went there."

Abbott looked at Jen. "You think... Bess?"

"What happened to you?" asked Jen.

"A monster. A madman. Tried to kill me in the mansion. But I escaped." She dried her eyes. "I'm afraid she went there."

"Who is this monster?" Jen asked.

Then Abbott interrupted. "Where is this mansion?"

The young girl gave Abbott and Jen directions, and they were off.

Winding their way through Guy Town, they came to a mansion set back from a tall metal gate from the street.

"This looks like it," Abbott stated.

"Don't you think we should find Smyth?" Jen asked.

"No time. If Bess is in that horrid place, we have to find her fast. You go look for him while I find Bess."

* * * *

A door creaked open behind Bess, followed by footsteps. She strained in her chair to see who it was.

He walked quietly around the bound woman until he came into Bess's sight.

She saw a man in his early thirties, his shabby genteel appearance contrasting starkly with the dark, sinister eyes that peered into her soul. He had a small black mustache and carried a small black leather case that a doctor might use for medicine and small instruments.

Bess knew at once that she was a lassie in serious trouble.

He didn't say a word and approached her, holding her head in his hand, tilting it gently, staring into her green, fear-filled eyes. She could see he enjoyed her frightened look.

"Do you like the guest I provided you in your room?" he said, pointing over his shoulder at the bloody body of Brannan hanging on the wall.

Bess could only shake her head in dread.

"So," he began, "shall we get better acquainted? My name is Mr. Jack Kelly," he said as he approached Bess with a tarnished scalpel gleaming in the oil light.

CHAPTER TWELVE

Once Abbott was in the mansion, he found himself in a confusing labyrinth. Doors that led nowhere, hallways going up and down and seemed to double back on themselves, and staircases that led to dead ends.

Perplexed in his search for Bess, he approached a door that he thought led to a lower floor.

It was locked.

Frustrated by the confusing search for Bess in the maze of the mansion, he kicked in the door. Shocked, he saw Bess tied to a chair with a threatening man hovering over her, a sharp instrument raised in his hand. A body was hanging in front of her, gently swaying and obviously dead.

Bess screamed. Abbott drew his pistol, his finger hovering over the trigger. But before he could shoot, the man ran to the wall of the room and was immediately swallowed up, as if the wall had opened and closed behind him.

"What the bloody hell was that?" Abbott cried, his voice echoing in the silent room. Then he hurried to Bess, untying her restraints. "How? What? Did he hurt you?"

Bess could only nod, and then threw her arms around Abbott. "That was him," she cried through her tears. "That was the Ripper!"

"Now we don't know that for sure," Abbott said, soothing her with soft words. "He could be just another deranged madman." He looked around the room, shivering as he stared at the bloody body of the bounty hunter. "And very sinister. In a rather menacing place."

"Where did he go?" asked Bess, still shaking from the experience.

"It was the damnedest thing I've ever seen. The wall seemed to swallow him up. Let's investigate it."

"No!" Bess pleaded. "Please. Let's leave this horrid place."

Abbott agreed, his own nerves frayed by the terrifying encounter.

* * * *

"Smyth! Smyth!" Jen shouted, waving her arms as she spotted him across the street. Dodging a horse-drawn carriage, she ran up to the Brit. "Come with me. Bess and Abbott could be in trouble. Hurry!"

Jen explained the situation as they raced towards the mansion.

Minutes later, they stood at the front door. Jen nodded to Smyth, who pushed it open. He surveyed the lobby and decided to enter one of the doors at the far end.

"Where do you think they might be?" Jen asked.

"Well, one door is as good as another," Smyth replied as they moved on.

Over the next twenty minutes, they were confronted with a confusing maze of doors, stairways, and baffling corridors.

"Smyth," Jen pleaded. "Let's split up. This is getting us nowhere."

Smyth didn't like the idea, but conceded that it would double their chances of finding their friends. He opened the door to his right, and Jen took the one to her left.

He had barely entered his door when he heard Jen scream.

Rushing towards the source of the scream, he saw an open trapdoor leading to a darkened pit with the sound of frantic splashing. He looked down a dozen feet into the pit and heard Jen cry, "Help me! Help me, Smyth!"

The pit was filling with water, rising slowly around her.

"Get me out of here!" she screamed.

"I can't reach you from here," Smyth said in frustration. "I need to find a way down to you."

Smyth searched frantically for a way to get to Jen. He tried every door and rushed down every maze. The dimly lit corridors didn't help much.

He was about to climb a set of stairs when he saw light coming from a crack in the wall next to him. He placed his hand on the sliver of light and realized it was part of a wall that was ajar.

A door? He thought.

He pushed on it, revealing a long and oil lamp-lit corridor.

Hoping it would lead to Jen's pit, he hurried down the corridor. Suddenly, a man with a long sword appeared from a door to his left and swung at him, barely missing Smyth's throat. Smyth drew his pistol, but the man bolted down the corridor. Smyth wanted to pursue him, but knew he had to get to Jen first.

The attack gave him an idea. He searched the corridor as he went, looking for any doors he could open.

He found one, opened it, and found himself just above Jen, who was now neck-deep in water.

"Hang in there," Smyth shouted as the water poured into Jen's pit.

He reached in, offering his hand. "Grab it!"

She grabbed his hand, and he pulled her through the door.

"Are you alright?"

"Yes," she said, spitting out water. "Just a bit wet." She didn't let go of his hand. "Thank you."

"Come. Let's find Abbott and Bess and get out of this... this, whatever it is."

"How, without getting into more traps this place has?"

"The same way I was able to save you," Smyth said. "Through the secret passage. Come on."

CHAPTER THIRTEEN

Smyth and Jen hurried through the corridor, their ears attuned to any sounds of Abbott or Bess.

It didn't take long.

They heard a gunshot from the other side of the passage wall, near an exit door. "That might be Abbott," Smyth figured. He opened the door and surprised Abbott, who immediately turned his pistol on him.

"Hold! It's me, old man!"

"Blimey, Smyth! You scared me senseless! Where the bloody hell did you come from?"

"This hell hole is riddled with secret passages," Smyth replied. "Hopefully, we'll use this door to get out of here. Hurry."

The chosen door did lead to the outside, and now safely in a garden, Smyth asked Abbott, "Who were you shooting at?"

"A man. He attacked us with a sword."

"Did you hit him?" Jen asked.

"No. He moved too quickly. Before I could get off another shot, you appeared and surprised me. When I turned back, he was gone."

"Can you describe him?" Jen asked.

Bess interrupted. "He's the Ripper."

"How do you know that?" Smyth replied.

"He told me his name. Jack Kelly."

"Like I said, that doesn't prove anything," Abbott replied.

"What I'd like to know," Bess asked, "is what in God's name is that insane asylum?"

Smyth was quiet, lost in thought. Then he said, "Bess may be right. It fits the Ripper's MO."

"How so?" asked Abbott.

"The Ripper thrived on the fear and terror of his victims," Smyth began. "A manifestation of the psychological torment experienced by his victims. This mansion, this 'murder hotel', if you could call it, was designed to instill a sense of fear and helplessness, a sense of isolation, fear, and despair. As I said, it fits the Ripper's MO. His Modus Operandi. Those secret passages allowed him to move around undetected and surprise his victims once they were lured in for whatever reason."

"Hmmm...And within the safe space of this mansion," Abbott added, "he could perform his horrid murders safely and securely, like Mary Jane Kelly's slaughter in Whitehall - is last and most gruesome murder."

"It all fits," Smyth remarked. "This and his ability to just sail away from London after the last murder, as Jen speculated." He paused a beat. "My money is on Jack Kelly. He's the Ripper."

"And he's still loose," Jen added.

"He's bottled up in there, now," Smyth stated. "I'm going back and find him."

"Not without me," Bess declared.

"Yes. Without you – or Jen. Both of you go back to the hotel. Get some shoes."

"There you go, Smyth. Giving orders again," she shot back.

"Please, Bess. Listen to me at least this one time."

Bess clenched her toes and stared at her bloodstained feet. "OK. But Jen and I will wait here."

"Agreed." He turned to Abbott. "Charles? Will you join me?"

Abbott nodded. "Let's end this thing."

CHAPTER FOURTEEN

Smyth and Abbott, their guns drawn, moved back into the hidden passage in search of Kelly.

 "Where do you think he may be?" asked Abbott.

"If he's not here in the passages, he could be anywhere. Perhaps a hidden room he uses."

"How do we find that?"

"We'll have to split up. You continue to search the hidden passages and I'll start snooping around the mazes and rooms."

"Be careful, Smyth," said Abbott. "This creature could pop out anywhere, not to mention the traps he sets."

Once they split up, Smyth entered yet another maze, making note of where he was and looking for doors and points of orientation. He came upon a door that opened to a stairway. Hoping Abbott was somewhere near him in a passage, he climbed the stairs softly and – he hoped - noiselessly, reaching the top of a landing. He cautiously felt the strength of the landing with his foot. Satisfied that all was stable and not a trap, he reached forward to open the door.

Immediately, Kelly threw himself at Smyth, that gleaming scalpel in his hand. They both tumbled down the stairs, back into the door to the maze.

Smyth hit his head hard against the door and was wedged between it and the maze entrance. He was momentarily dazed.

Kelly took this opportunity to sit his full weight on Smyth's chest and placed the scalpel against Smyth's throat.

"Game over, old man," he croaked. "I win, Mr. Smyth."

'You know me?"

"I read the papers about your hunt for me."

Kelly pressed the edge of the blade to Smyth's throat. "The hunt is over."

"No. It's not!" a stern voice boomed behind them.

Kelly turned around just as Abbott cold cocked him across the head.

"Told you to be careful, Smyth," Abbott grinned. "Lucky for you, I found you."

Smyth came to his feet and said, "Let's get him up and join the women."

Outside in the garden, Bess was all grins. She walked up to Kelly and said, "Remember me?" and punched him straight in the face.

"That's enough, Bess," Smyth said.

"He had it coming," she growled.

Smyth smiled and shook his head. "Yes. He did. But now, let's get him to the police station."

Kelly, rubbing his bleeding nose, looked at Jen and smiled. "Hello, sis."

Jen nodded, pulled Abbott's gun from his belt, and shot Kelly between the eyes.

Kelly dropped dead, in a heap and the others stood aghast.

"What?...What?..." stammered Bess.

Abbott and Smyth stood there dumbfounded.

When Smyth recovered from the shock, he asked, "Why did you shoot him!?"

"Don't get any ideas of arresting me, Smyth. You don't have jurisdiction," Jen snarled.

"Answer the question," Smyth replied. "Why did you kill him?"

"Had to." She handed Abbott back his pistol. "He went rogue, and the Society needed him out."

"What Society?" asked a befuddled Abbott.

"The Crimson Crows. We are a Society of Secretive Assassins."

"I never heard of them," said Smyth.

"And you never will," Jen said, looking down at the dead body of Kelly. "We had to stop him. If he was caught, he could give away the Society."

"So, your Society is filled with maniacs like Kelly." Bess stated flatly.

"No. We kill on contract. He killed for pleasure." She paused and said, "Do what you want. Believe what you want." And walked away.

"What do we tell the authorities?" asked Bess.

"That we found the serial killer and he was shot defending ourselves - and tell them to pick up the body," Smyth said. "What else can we say? Jen was right. No jurisdiction. And who's to believe what Jen said?" He shook his head. "Secret society."

Smyth sighed. "I can use a drink. Anyone want to join me?"

Johnathan Smyth: Cowboy Sleuth

Series Titles

BOOK 1 'The Case of the Screaming Tunnel'

BOOK 2 'The Case of the Lost Ship In The Desert'

BOOK 3 'The Case of the Red Ghost Camel'

BOOK 4 'The Case of the Prescott Tunnels'

BOOK 5 'The Case of the Deathly Water Babies of Pyramid Lake

BOOK 6 'The Case of the Murder Mansion'

A Note to the Reader

Obviously, this is a work of fiction.

No one knows what really happened to Jack the Ripper and multiple theories have been set forth about who the Ripper was and what he may or may not have done after the gruesome murder and dismemberment of Mary Kelly.

I have stitched together some of the theories in this work.

1. That the Ripper was a merchant seaman that visited London port not far from Whitehall and committed the Ripper murders, then left on his steamer back to America.

2. Once in America, he was responsible for the serial murders recorded at the time.

3. Of those suspects, I chose H.H. Holmes, America's first known serial killer, and his reported use of a 'murder castle'. Holmes' technique was to turn his hotel into a "murder castle" which was full of booby traps and torture devices where he would skin and dissect his victims. In fact, you could argue that H.H. Holmes was the inspiration behind the modern "SAW" movie franchise.

4. As far as being a rogue member of the Society of Assassins, I thought that to be a fitting explanation and end for the Jonathan Smyth saga.

I hope you enjoyed the final wrap up of the series.